The
Curtain Call

Beyond the Stars

Table of Contents

CHAPTER ONE

Los Angeles - same evening

"I'm on the way. Please bring your checkbook."

Rupert refrained from groaning; he knew Daven would pay him back without being asked. "Oh god, the early transfer fees. How much is the damage this time?"

"Three hundred thousand. Needless to say-"

"I know."

Daven paused. "That's per deed, by the way."

"Of course it is." Rupert tried not to grimace at his wife, who was standing a few feet away after having zipped up her husband's little suitcase.

"We're coming up the driveway, now," Daven grunted.

"Be right there. Thanks."

Rupert hung up and turned to his wife. "I'm so sorry about this, Millie."

"It's alright," she said quickly. "I've already said a hundred times that I'm glad the boys are coming."

Rupert noticed her eyes were wet and red all of a sudden, and he quickly wiped away the emerging tears and hugged her tight. "I'll call our movers first thing in the morning to clear out the basement and set those rooms to rights again. Don't worry, you won't have to do a thing except let them in and point the way-"

"That's not what I'm upset about. You know we have three empty bedrooms upstairs, right?"

"Please don't start, Millie. I don't like it either, but they have to live downstairs. That's the law."

She pulled away abruptly. "I wonder who's fault *that* is."

"You're not being fair. Sweetheart, can you go get the checkbook while I take this suitcase outside? Please?"

"I'm not letting them live in the basement, Rupe. It's cold, and dark. They're Hank's kids, not some old luggage we can just leave in a corner and forget about until they're needed."

Rupert almost retorted something bitter about her not feeling the same about their previous servants, but instead, he stepped forward to gently wipe her hair off her face and lay his hands on her shoulders. "Sweetie, you know we can't have them living upstairs. I'm not going to fight you about it. Their rooms will be in the basement, and that's final."

"Final for you, maybe. Not for me. You know Theo's afraid of the dark. He wouldn't even go into the basement of his own house in broad daylight. Hank's going to be pissed when he hears about this, law or not. You're his best friend, and those are your godsons!"

Rupert ignored the sudden lump in his throat and let a dark edge creep into his tone. "I have to go. The basement needs to be ready for them by the time I get back. If it's not, they'll be sleeping on boxes and luggage until it is, and I'll lock them down there if necessary. Are we clear?"

Millie eyed her husband curiously, and her expression softened. "From your reaction to me mentioning Hank, I'm guessing the rumors are true."

"What rumors?" he asked needlessly, and that was all the answer she needed. Her eyes glistened again.

"Oh god. Do they know?"

Rupert hesitated, but ultimately declined to answer outright. "Babe, you know I love Floyd and Theo as much as I love our own kids. That's exactly why I'm insisting we follow the law. They could be taken away if we don't. Not worth the risk."

"Fine. Basement it is. But we're taking their dogs in, too," she replied with steely determination.

"Of course." He leaned over and kissed her on forehead. "Seriously, I've got to go. Love you."

Richmond, Virginia

Floyd had tossed and turned all night long, more restless than he'd been in months. When his alarm went off at 6am, he couldn't believe that he'd only gotten about an hour of sleep while his brother had slept soundly and peacefully for at least 7 hours straight.

"Theo," he called, their usual morning ritual starting a bit early; usually Floyd was only coherent after hitting the snooze button half a dozen times.

"*Theo* . Theody. Samantha. Theo I am. I am Theo. Am I Theo?"

"*Shut up, Floyd.*"

Floyd started to sing his usual morning song - something from Sesame Street he'd heard ages ago, but with some variation of "Theo" substituting every word - when the shadow of someone walking up and standing in front of the door stopped him in his tracks. He laid back down and covered himself up entirely, just in time. The door shuddered opened with a squeal, and then slowly the room became brighter and brighter.

"Floyd. I know you're awake. Get dressed and come with me, kiddo."

Floyd pulled the blanket down just enough to peek out. He hadn't been in trouble in weeks, but that tone of voice indicated otherwise, and he started to tremble.

"What did I do?" he asked nervously. There was no reply; the door shut again and the shadow stayed put. He looked over at his brother.

"What did you do?" Theo asked fearfully.

"Nothing." He got up anyway, and quickly threw on his clothes and shoes, and also a jacket so that he could pretend the cold was causing shivers instead of anxiety.

"Floyd..."

"It's okay, Theody. I got this." Floyd was far more nervous than he would admit as he pulled open the door. Lester Boyd was still waiting on the other side, looking grim.

"You're not in trouble, but you're not going to like what's next, either. You got to promise me you'll keep your mouth shut until it's over. I want absolute silence, or else. Got me?"

Floyd stared at him in dismay. "Is that, like...a threat?"

"If it has to be. Follow me."

He led the bewildered teenager to a building on the far edge of campus, way past the point Floyd was allowed to go, and yes - it was damned cold. Now he was shaking from anxiety *and* the chill. The sun was turning the sky purple above the tree line.

"You're freaking me out, Lester," he finally said. "I mean, Mr. Boyd. Sorry."

Lester turned towards him at the door of the plain building, which clearly housed some kind of administrative function. "I'm dead serious, Floyd. Silence unless you are asked to speak directly, in which case it will probably be yes or no questions. And you're going to stick to yes or no. Clear?"

"Wait, can't you just give-"

"Floyd."

Floyd put his hands in his pockets and shivered. "Yes. It's clear."

"Thank you. Hands out of your pockets, stand up straight. Let's go."

They forged ahead and quickly turned into a room which could only belong to someone very high up in the hierarchy of the school, because the room made Lester Boyd's office look like a dilapidated shack.

Before Floyd could fully take in his surroundings, a heavy door on the far side opened with a loud click. When Rupert and Daven walked through, Floyd nearly pissed himself in surprise. He was vaguely aware of Lester tightly squeezing his arm to keep him in place as a third man emerged after Rupert, but Floyd didn't know him.

"Quiet, Floyd," Lester grumbled warningly. "Stay still."

The third man came forward and stood in front of Floyd. "I'm Mr. Sebastian, the president of this school. We haven't had the pleasure of meeting yet."

"Pleasure?" Floyd blurted hotly, and Lester squeezed his arm painfully, but subtly enough that the other men in the room didn't notice. Then he let go, and Floyd felt himself wishing he hadn't, because he didn't know if he could resist the urge to flee from the room as quickly as possible.

Floyd didn't look at his two "uncles," but he had turned bright red at the first sight of them. Daven had noticed it, of course, and didn't approach him as planned. Lester realized Daven had expected a much happier welcome, but he was about to be sorely disappointed.

Mr. Sebastian looked at Lester and nodded, then back to Floyd. "Floyd, the deeds to you and Theo have been transferred to Rupert Aster. You'll both be leaving our school today to travel back to Los Angeles with him and take up residence in his home. How long do you think you'll need to pack?"

So much for those yes or no questions, Floyd thought idly. He forced himself to remain polite. "I want to stay here. Theo will as well, so no need to ask him. Thank you, though."

The room went dead silent, except for Rupert's sharp intake of breath, and Lester felt rather than saw the hot glare from Daven directed at him specifically.

Sebastian gathered his wits and then spoke again. "I'm afraid you don't have any say in the matter. Return to your room and pack, please. As quickly as you can manage. Thank you, Mr. Boyd."

Daven stepped forward. "Just a minute, please. I want to talk to Floyd before he goes."

Sebastian hesitated. "Rupert is his deed holder, so technically you need his permi-"

"He can talk to him," Rupe interrupted firmly. "Got a room they can use?"

Daven stood a respectful distance away from Hank's oldest son and tried not to let his own disappointment and surprise dictate what he said next.

"Floyd, please explain why you would want to stay here. I'm not understanding why you would say such a hurtful thing. We've all but moved heaven and earth to get you back."

Floyd stared at him stonily, all defiance and stubbornness. "I refuse to believe you're that stupid," he nearly spit out. "You know why!"

Daven held his hands out in a *what the hell are you talking about* gesture. "No, I don't. Why don't you tell me?"

"Go fuck yourself. You act like we'd be going home, like you're doing us a favor...but you want us to be *Rupert's servants!*"

"You're going to be servants no matter what, Floyd. Might as well be with someone you trust, and who loves you. You're extremely lucky it all worked out this way."

Floyd laughed a little. "Lucky. Yeah. I *don't* trust him, and I definitely don't trust you. I repeat: go fuck yourself. How much did you pay for us, anyway?"

"Three hundred thousand dollars. Each. But Rupert and I would have spent every last penny, and begged and borrowed if we had to, in order to get you out of here. Your dad, by the way, wanted exactly this. So don't tell me you aren't coming. I won't accept it, because it dishonors his efforts and sacrifice."

Floyd seemed truly taken aback by that - deeply stunned, actually - and had no immediate reply.

"Listen, Floyd," Daven said quietly, in desperate surrender. "Whatever's happened, we can talk about it later. I've got a plane waiting on the tarmac for you at Richmond Airport. Your dogs are inside, waiting for you boys. I'm not going to let them be disappointed."

Daven was inexpressibly relieved to see Floyd visibly calm down at that. "My...my dogs?"

"Yes. Starsky and Hutch are not even 20 miles away. I had to leave Shannon at home, but she's waiting for you, too. I know you have questions about your dad, and I'll answer them. But not here. I want to get you the hell out of here as quickly as possible, before Lester can change his mind."

Again, Floyd was stunned. "What does Lester have to do with this?"

Daven replied calmly, "He owns your deeds. I've already given over the check to pay for them, and Rupert's got provisional custody...but until you sign the transfer, he can change his mind. Which he might do, by the way, if you continue to behave like this."

It was obvious Floyd had no idea Lester held his deed, and - exactly as Daven hoped - the knowledge quickly obliterated Floyd's warm feelings towards the man.

"You mean he didn't ever bother to tell us that he *owned* us? This whole time? What the fuck! That's sick."

"Language, Floyd, please. He didn't bother to tell me, either. I just found out today. All Bonded Retainers have the right to refuse transfer, or request one, if they feel their personal safety is in peril. It's one of the many laws put in place for your protection. You and Theo will have to sign the new deeds and approve your own transfer. I'm asking you to please do that, and not fight about it."

"I'm not signing anything until you tell me where my dad is and what happened to him," Floyd decided firmly. "Right now, in this room. Not later."

Daven had gone over this exact scenario with Rupert on the plane. He knew that was going to be Floyd's reaction all along, and was prepared. But that still didn't make it any easier. He swallowed a few times and then took a deep breath.

"No. Not here."

The door open and Mr. Sebastian stepped in. "Gentlemen, time to wrap it up. Floyd, out."

Floyd went instantly and without argument, to Daven's surprise and relief.

"Mr. Johansson, I hope you convinced the boy this is for the best."

"I don't know. I hope."

They went back into the office, where Floyd took the new deed from Lester and read over it a few times. Then he looked back up - pointedly aiming a question directly at Rupert, not Daven.

"Where are my dogs?"

Rupert answered nervously, having just heard a brief explanation from Lester in the meantime exactly what the hell was going on between Floyd and Daven. "Your very bad dogs are on the plane at Richmond Airfield. They made a nice snack out of the new upholstery somewhere over Kansas when we weren't looking, but I know you'll ensure they behave on the way back."

He thought that would cheer Floyd up, but it did nothing. He was as determined and steely-eyed as he'd ever been.

"Haven't agreed to go back yet. I have conditions. I understand we have to live in the basement, technically, but Theo gets a room to sleep in upstairs at night."

Rupert started a little, then nodded. "Agreed."

"Rupe-" interrupted Dav.

"No, it's fine. Theo sleeps upstairs when we don't have guests, and the pool house if we do. Any other conditions?"

"He starts homeschooling again."

"No, Floyd." That was from Daven. "Absolutely not. There are laws Rupert has to follow in order to keep custody of you boys. We can bend some to your needs, but this isn't one of them."

Floyd nodded. "Fine. No corporal punishment for him, then."

Rupert nodded readily. "Or you, Floyd. You have my word. If that's all, please go ahead and sign so we can get the hell out of here."

"It's not all. You're going to tell me and Theo what happened with dad. Not him." Floyd threw a glare at Daven, then back to Rupert. "That brings me to my last condition. You will never ask me to assist Daven in any way, or even speak to him. At the dinner table, at functions, whatever. I won't do it. After today, the bastard doesn't exist as far as I'm concerned."

"A moment, gentlemen, please," said Lester as he stepped into the tense little circle and took Floyd's arm, then pulled him into the same room where he'd spoken with Daven earlier and slammed the door behind them.

"Owners aren't allowed to touch their servants without their consent, Mr. Boyd," Floyd warned as he jerked his elbow away.

Lester froze. This was the exact reason he'd never told the boys he had their deeds.

"Floyd, calm down. I've told you before, Daven doesn't deserve to be treated that way. If you only knew the shit he's been through in the past eight months trying to get you freed, you'd be kissing his ass. Get back in there and apologize before I cane the crap out of you as a parting gift."

"Do it," Floyd challenged. "I'm not apologizing."

The door opened again and Daven pushed in impatiently. "Let him go, Mr. Boyd. It's alright. I agreed to those terms. Floyd, it's time to make a decision. Come on. Out, both of you."

With a final glare at Lester, Floyd strode from the room. "I'm not signing until Theo does. Mr. Sebastian, will you kindly walk me back to my room? I don't know how to get there from here."

"Mr. Boyd will walk you back."

"I'm not going anywhere with him."

"Mr. Boyd will walk you back," Mr. Sebastian repeated patiently. "Mr. Johansson and Mr. Aster will depart for the airport now and wait for you there. You never told me how long it will take you to pack."

"Half an hour, at the most. If we decide to leave, that is."

"Very well. I'll remain here with the deeds. Good day, gentlemen."

ONE HOUR LATER

Floyd had already known, of course, that Theo would instantly capitulate, no matter how his big brother felt about Daven. He hated being trained as a house servant, and was happy and energetic as the car pulled up to take them and Lester Boyd to Richmond Airfield, with the few belongings they still had between in one bag and the new deeds in a sealed envelope in the other.

After a few minutes, Theo spoke up. "Aren't you happy, Floyd? Oh my god. We're going home."

"You mean to Rupert's house. As his servants."

"Servants, students, whatever. Same thing. We practically grew up there. It's like home." Floyd fell silent while Theo leaned up against him. "Uncle Dav made this happen, Floyd."

Lester watched the elder Bancroft through the rearview mirror. He didn't like what he saw as Floyd slouched back further, the look in his eyes increasingly dark and lifeless by the second.

"You're right about that, Theo. We can thank Daven for all of this."

CHAPTER TWO

Richmond, Virginia

7:00am

Daven didn't feel anything as he and Rupert were escorted from the BRTSM's administration building to the airport. Perhaps it was numbness, or weariness, or he had exhausted his bank of emotions for the month...or, he knew, he felt too much and simply couldn't process it all. Not that it was a huge surprise, really. He knew Floyd was upset with him long before this, considering how the teenager had acted towards him back in late March, but it was the unexpected depth of the hostility that had shocked him to the core.

Rupert was shocked too; perhaps even more so. He'd had no idea Floyd harbored any ill-will towards Daven at all. He wanted to ask about it as they drove to the airport, but Dav wasn't ready, if the expression on his face was any judge of things. The man was clearly still wondering how the older boy had ended up telling him to go fuck himself with no apparent provocation.

So they rode in silence for a while, until Daven suddenly decided to open up.

"Rupe...it's a good thing the deeds went to you. I can't even fathom what would be happening right now if they had gone to me. Floyd would've refused to leave."

"Sure seems like it. While you were talking to him, Lester whispered to me that Floyd thinks you turned Hank in. Did you know that?"

Daven turned and stared at Rupe for a moment. "No. I knew he was upset that I didn't defend Hank after he was arrested, but...what the hell gave him the idea I turned him in?"

"I think it's pretty clear that Lester Boyd brainwashed him. Probably got to Theo, too."

Daven thought about what he had heard behind the door a few minutes ago: Lester telling Floyd he should be grateful to Daven for trying to save them. Trying to make him apologize. The man definitely didn't do this.

"It wasn't Lester. Had to be something he heard on the news. Remember Hailey dropped that alleged report that I was behind all this back in March? Floyd might have caught wind of it."

"Oh...shit. Well, you can easily disprove that now. Show Floyd all the lawsuits for slander she's been hit with in the last few years. Can't believe it took that long for her to lose her license."

"Hmm. Yes. Just so you know, I've asked Lester Boyd to move to Los Angeles and work for us. He turned it down right away, but I know he'll change his mind in a few weeks. We need to start thinking of a position for him."

Rupert's jaw dropped. "I'm sorry, I thought I heard you say you *asked Lester Boyd to move to Los Angeles to work for us.* Come again?"

Daven nodded, but he didn't look at Rupe. His thoughts were far away, on another planet almost. "I can't tell you why, but he knows."

"I can't accept that, Dav," Rupert said sternly.

"You'll have to, I'm afraid. I'll explain when I can. It might be a while. First things first. I was planning to tell the boys about Hank, but looks like you agreed to be the messenger for that. What are you going to say?"

Rupert rapped on the privacy glass in the car, and it rolled down a few inches. "Martinez. Have the driver pull up at the Waffle House off the next exit. You guys can go get a bite and leave us alone in the car for a bit."

"Yes, sir. Call me when you want us back in."

"I will."

The glass rolled back up as they pulled into the restaurant. Once the men had left the car, Rupert turned back around to glare at Daven.

"Okay, Dav. We need to have a serious come-to-Jesus. Look, I didn't say anything when you suddenly foisted the boys upon me as servants, even though I already have three kids. Now I'm going to have five, and four dogs. I wrote that $600,000 check without blinking-"

"I'm paying you back when we get to the airport."

"-after I barely whimpered when you met secretly with Harmon without informing me. I fought with my wife over this, for you and those boys. And yes, I'll take the last-second responsibility of telling them about Hank even though I'm not prepared, because you never bothered to tell me Floyd was pissed at you. What I won't do is sit back and let you treat me like I'm some kind of untrustworthy blabbermouth. I'm flying home in an hour with two traumatized teenagers who think their Uncle Dav just had their dad executed by their own government, while you get to disappear off the radar for a week and let me and my family deal with the nuclear fallout that these poor boys are about to experience. Do you realize what a massive PR nightmare this is all going to be? And you want Lester Boyd there now, too, whom Floyd *also* hates? I deserve to know what's going on, and you have no longer have any right to keep it from me. So start talking."

Daven's expression never changed during this tirade, which only made it worse for Rupert.

"No," Dav answered calmly, folding his hands in his lap and cocking his head slightly at his right hand man.

Rupert was appalled. "No? Did you just say...no?"

"Correct. But perhaps what I should've said is *not right now*. Maybe you'll figure it out on your own, if you calm down and think hard enough about what's going on and why I would do all these things. Take your time, we don't have to be at the airport for a while."

"I don't understand you. I don't understand any of this. Jesus Christ. All this subterfuge. You're Hank, reincarnated." Rupert shook his head and fell silent, wondering if his anger could possibly set the car on fire in its intensity. He refused to think about the situation at first, preferring to silently fume and think about how to write his resignation letter. He had just composed it all inside his head when the unexpected occurred.

"Holy shit." He sat straight up in his seat. "Lester is cooperating with the FBI. You knew he was going to turn against Colbert. You said so months ago."

"Hmm. I do recall saying that, come to think of it." There was a slight sparkle in his eye now, and he totally unconscious of it, but Rupert knew that look like he knew two plus two equals four.

"Is it really necessary to ask him to come to Los Angeles?"

"Silly question. Come on, Rupe, you're smarter than that."

Because Lester would never be able to find a job again in Urbanes territory after this, Rupert realized. He pulled his mind away from the topic for a moment and studied their driver and Martinez through the windows of the Waffle House; they appeared to have just received their bill. Rupert picked up his phone and quickly dialed Daven's guard.

"Come to the car, please. Just you, only for a moment, thanks."

Daven looked sideways at him. "What are you doing?"

Rupert dug out his wallet. "Paying their bill, of course. Want anything to go?" He took out two twenty dollar bills and handed them to Martinez, asked him to grab them some food, then turned and smiled sadly at Daven when they were alone again.

"Alright, so I get it. You know what? You've learned a lot from Hank about strategy. I'm impressed. But I'm also worried as shit, you must know that."

"Of course. I have no intention of getting myself executed, though."

"Well, it's a pretty strange state of affairs when I can say something like that is the best news I've heard all day. Thank you."

Daven chuckled a little. "I wonder what Hank would think of us right now if he could hear us. Probably shaking his head and muttering *amateurs*. He would have solved this whole crisis months ago under different circumstances, without breaking a sweat."

Rupert looked at him in disbelief. "You think too highly of him, Dav. Always have. I loved him too, but *solved* this? Really? No, he *caused* this. Don't forget that."

Daven was quiet again, and Rupert broke the silence a minute later. "So, when I tell the boys...I think Floyd won't want you there at all. Or maybe there, just not saying anything."

"I don't know. Ask him. We should go."

Rupert picked up his phone again, but paused halfway through dialing Martinez's number. "So, one more question. While I'm going back to H.A., you're heading to Philadelphia. Are you getting arrested, or not? Tell me honestly."

"That's up to the president. You already know I breached the confidentiality agreement. Technically, they can charge me with conspiracy. But I don't think they will."

"You don't think? That doesn't make me feel better."

Dav shrugged, so Rupert went back to his phone and finished dialing the number.

Lester looked back at Floyd again through the rearview mirror. Theo was now sound asleep on his brother's shoulder, mouth open and breathing heavily. Floyd was wide awake, and he looked right back at Lester.

"About five minutes away, Floyd. You okay?"

Floyd ignored him and turned to stare out the window.

"I can tell you on the plane why I kept that secret, if you're willing to listen," Lester said quietly, although he doubted he could wake Theo even if he shouted it at the top of his lungs.

Nothing from Floyd. Lester sighed and looked up to watch a large cargo jet coming down the glide slope just overhead. It seemed like the landing gear could have thumped the top of the car if the pilot had dipped down just a few feet lower. Less than two minutes later they pulled into the private hangar, and the driver got out and shut the door. Lester turned all the way around in his seat.

"Floyd. Harmon was supposed to get your deeds. Your dad insisted that I get them instead so I could turn them over to

Daven after a year, because he was convinced Harmon would be in jail by now."

"Is he?"

"No. Why you're going to Rupert instead, five months early, I don't know, but I have an idea and you should be damned grateful about it."

Floyd shrugged. "Don't care. Doesn't explain why you kept it a secret."

"Your dad insisted on it. He thought you wouldn't trust me if you knew. He was right, of course, as you've just proven. He knew you too well to risk it."

Floyd shrugged again. "Like I said, I don't care. Wait...what do you mean, *knew* me?"

"What?"

"*Knew me* . Past tense. Why did you say it like that?" Floyd's voice was suddenly pitched an octave higher, and when Lester didn't immediately respond, he grabbed the door handle and bolted out of the car towards the plane.

Lester followed in a panic, but he was too late, and he arrived to all kinds of yelling inside the cabin. He poked his head around the bulkhead and saw that Daven had his hands out in a defensive gesture, while Rupert was holding Floyd's arms in a bear hug from behind.

"Calm down, Floyd. Hey, calm down," Rupert said soothingly, over and over.

Daven glared at Lester. "What the hell did you say to him?"

"Where's my dad, you traitorous fuck?" Floyd nearly spit at Daven.

Daven didn't look at him. "Mr. Boyd, go get Theo, please. Bring him up so we can talk." Then he gestured to his guards and the stunned pilots. "All of you need to leave, please. Right now. We've got this."

Lester went back to the car with a sickly-pounding heart and woke up Theo. "Hey, kiddo. Up and at 'em. You've got to get on the plane to help calm your brother. Come on."

"What? Is he having a panic attack?"

"Not yet, but sure looks like he's on the way. Come on and let's try to help him out of it."

Too late. Floyd was already lying on the floor, heaving in fruitless deep breaths, eyes wild. Theo went immediately to his side and pushed his hood back and out of his face.

"Do we need to call medics?" asked Rupert quickly. He was scared, not having seen Floyd before in this state, although he'd heard about it.

"No," Daven responded, going down on a knee on the side of Floyd opposite Theo and putting a hand on the boy's chest. "He'll be okay. You remember how to breathe, Floyd. Come on, start counting."

"Get off me," Floyd growled, and Daven stood back up quickly.

Theo looked around the cabin. "Can you guys leave us alone, please? I've got this. He just needs some breathing room."

They didn't move, then Theo asked again, not as politely, but more pleadingly.

"Come on," Daven finally said to his little entourage. "Off the plane. Let's go."

"You okay now?" Theo asked some time later, when it was obvious Floyd was perfectly fine. Physically, anyway.

"Yeah. Thanks for your help, Theody." Floyd started to sit up, then laid back down again. "Can you go get Lester?"

Theo stood up and did as asked; Floyd was upright and in a chair by the time they returned, looking grim.

"Can you sit, please?" Floyd asked Lester, very politely.

"Of course. You look a hell of a lot better than you did twenty minutes ago. Thank god."

"I understand now why you didn't tell us about the deeds. I'm sorry I freaked out on you."

"You are literally the last person in the universe who needs to apologize for anything, Floyd."

Floyd took a bottle of water from the little table off to the side, and drank a few gulps. "Please tell us what happened to our dad. Theody, sit down."

Lester's heart lurched a little. "Yeah, you'd better sit. Thanks. I'm sorry, boys. Your dad is...he passed away in April. While he was in jail."

Theo stopped breathing for a few moments, then whined a little, but Floyd had no visible reaction. "How long have you known?"

"I just found out yesterday." Lester's voice broke, and he started to tear up. "That's why Daven and Rupert came to get you. They also found out yesterday, by the way."

Floyd gestured to Theo, who got up and sat in his lap, looking stunned and red-faced. Floyd put his arms around his little brother protectively and held on tightly.

"Did he get sick?" Floyd queried, his voice a bit muffled through Theo's mop of hair.

"Not sick. You remember he had a heart attack about six years ago?"

"Of course."

"That was a minor one. He had another one and this time, a big one, he couldn't be saved. Everybody tried, but...they really tried. They couldn't save him. I'm told he felt no pain at all and wasn't even aware of it. Happened in his sleep. He was...you may not believe it now, but it probably was for the best, because he was going to be in jail for a long time. And he would have been so desperately unhappy there."

"So he was found guilty."

"He admitted to his guilt, actually. So...do you understand what I mean by this maybe being for the best?"

Floyd nodded again, and went white as a sheet when Theo wailed a little.

"Thank you. Can you leave us alone, please?"

Lester got up, squeezed Floyd's shoulder, then patted Theo on the head and left the plane. Daven and Rupert were waiting expectantly, shivering at the foot of the stairs.

"Both of you, in the car," Lester ordered sternly. "We need to talk."

"You okay, Theody?"

Theo nodded. He was in shock, and quiet as a mouse for the past few minutes. "You always said he'd work himself to death, Floyd. Guess you were right."

"Yeah." Floyd was in shock, too. He hugged his brother a little tighter. "I feel like...I think I'm going to throw up?"

"Me, too."

Neither one of them did, though. They just held each other tightly, willing tears to come that stubbornly refused to emerge for now...the eye before the storm, as it were.

Daven burst out of the car, in total disbelief of what Lester had just done. It would be many hours before he realized it was the right thing, but right now? Nothing but fury. He turned around as Rupert got out of the car and slowly approached him.

"Calm down, Dav."

"You can't *possibly* agree with this bullshit?" Daven hissed.

"Keep your voice down."

"He actually had the nerve to blackmail me, and you're okay with it."

Rupert pulled his coat tighter around him and zipped it up. The day seemed to be getting colder as the sun rose, not warmer. "Not blackmail, Dav. A bargain."

"He said...he said he'd refuse to corroborate my testimony if I don't go along with this! It's unconscionable! Oh my god, you do agree with him. I can't believe it."

Rupe nodded. "Yeah, I do. I mean, I definitely thought he was completely insane at first, but if you think about it...what do the boys gain from knowing the truth? Nobody knows but us, and Harmon and literally all of three people in the government. I don't know if you remember, but Hank's death certificate does say heart attack."

Daven was nearly in a rage, his coat blowing around in the wind like dancing flames on the tarmac. "How the *hell* am I going to explain this to Salome and President Rickon?"

"You don't. They have no intention of ever letting the boys know the truth anyway. Why do you think there's no written record of anything that happened, hm? Especially if it's discovered that Colbert was the one who caused all this. Can you imagine how much that would damage them, and not to mention, Floyd and Theo?"

"I can't lie to them. I won't."

"You don't have to. Lester already did it for us."

"Did you put him up to this?" Daven asked accusingly.

"No! Are you fucking kidding me?" Rupert responded hotly, completely astonished. "How and when would I have possibly done that? I can't believe you would even say such a thing."

Daven shook his head, then surrendered. "Fine. I'm going to say goodbye to them, then I'm heading up to Philadelphia. We'll talk when I get back to Los Angeles. Don't even think of trying to contact me before that, and consider yourself lucky that I'm not firing you right here and now."

Daven stalked away and climbed the stairs to the plane, forcing himself to slow his breathing and his pace. It would do no good whatsoever to show the boys his current state of mind.

Floyd didn't look up as he came in, but Theo and the dogs did. Starsky was curled up in Theo's lap, while Hutch was shoved in next to Floyd on his seat, half-hanging over the side, tail wagging wildly as his human absently scratched his neck.

Daven kept a respectful distance, again, while keeping his tone gentle and reassuring. "Floyd. I just learned that you think I turned your dad in. My guess is you heard that on the news, or read something Hailey wrote. That explains why you're so upset with me. If it were true, I wouldn't blame you a bit. But it's not. We'll talk when I get back to Los Angeles on Saturday. My deepest condolences for the loss of your father. He was my best friend, and I swore to him that I would protect you and Theo for the rest of your lives if something happened to him."

Now Floyd spoke up, but his tone was hard. "So why does Rupert own our deeds, then?"

Daven pinched the bridge of his nose, and then took a step closer. "Because I'm not ready to be a father to you boys. I work too much, sleep too much, don't understand teenagers...there's a whole list of reasons why Rupert and Millie were a much better choice. Hank would have agreed, by the way. But my mission to protect you doesn't change because of that. I'm going to Philadelphia now for a few days, and the only thing I'll be working on is trying to cancel your servitude and free you completely. I'm dedicated to doing that at any cost, if it's possible."

Theo sat up, deeply interested now. "Is it possible?"

"I hope so, Theo. I really do. It's going to take a long time to work out, maybe months. In the meantime, you're going home with Rupert and the dogs to rest for a while, and then...well, we'll see. Be really nice to him, and be good. He loves you. So do I, by the way."

"Thank you, Uncle Dav," said Theo. Daven felt his heart glow a little, but it was tamped down again when he glanced at Floyd, who was still glowering and obviously felt no such gratitude for his father's best friend.

"See you soon, boys."

Daven left the plane and looked around for Rupert, who had gotten back in the car to get out of the cold. He beckoned him out with his finger. Rupert got back out, and stood in front of his boss, looking sullen and hurt.

"Yes, sir?"

"Don't call me that. Sorry I went off on you. I don't want to fire you. I just...this is a nightmare. Safe travels home. Oh, wait! The check."

Daven went to the trunk and opened his briefcase, and then wrote the check for $600,000 and quickly handed it over.

"Thanks, Dav. I was thinking that perhaps you should tell Salome that you didn't tell the boys about the execution, of course. They'll be grateful to hear it, and that might help you."

"Well, I need all the help I can get, so that's good advice. I still don't agree with it, though."

"You don't have to. Just accept it. Remember the boys gain nothing by the truth on this one."

"They don't gain anything, no, but I feel like we've lost our souls by doing it."

Rupert shrugged. "Maybe we have. I'm fine with it, for one. I suppose this means you're going to retract that job offer to Lester?"

"Obviously."

"Of course. Well. Good luck in Philadelphia."

Rupe opened the door and Daven got back in his own car; thankfully his driver had waited in order to prevent him and Lester from having to ride together. That would have been a veritable bloodbath.

As they both were driven away, Rupert heard a few barks emerging from the plane, followed by a loud thump and some stifled laughter. He smiled to himself, then walked into the hangar office where the flight crew was waiting.

"I think we're good to go, gentlemen and ladies. Sorry for the delay."

CHAPTER THREE

Los Angeles - 10 days later

"No, it's not like that," Rupert clarified, shifting his phone to the other ear. "Sorry, let me explain. Floyd's not defiant at all. He does everything we ask. Sometimes resentfully, but he always does it. I was referring to the way he protects his brother. I had to scold Theo for playing around with the gas stove, and Floyd came running in from god knows where, hell-bent on starting World War 3 about it. He acted like I was murdering Theo, when I was only trying to prevent him from blowing up the house."

"What did you do?" Daven asked with a huge yawn as he stretched and tried to wake up fully from having slept in so late. Again. The hotel's bed was way too comfortable for anything else.

"I sent him back to his room to calm down, and he cussed up a shitstorm the whole way down. You should have seen me trying not to laugh. The next morning he strode into the living room and announced that I must never raise my voice again to his brother, then proceeded to make us all an amazing breakfast and was perfectly polite. Never said a word the rest of the day. He might be the death of me before the new year,

37

Dav. I can't figure him out. He goes from being pitifully subservient one moment to blowing up at me the next, and it's not always about Theo. Speaking of which, the day *that* little brat takes an order without arguing, I'll be king of England and you'll be my queen. Floyd's spoiling him is only making it worse. Have to admit I cringe thinking back about how upset I'd get at Hank whenever he took his belt to them, but now I get it."

"No, you don't. This behavior is new. They never acted like that at my house, or at their own as far as I know. In all the days they spent with me I only had to make them stand in the corner a handful of times for fighting, but they were really little back then. They're such good kids otherwise. Hank was way too hard on them. I would even go so far as to say borderline abusive at times."

Rupert agreed with a harrumph. "Yeah. I wasn't going to say it, but...anyway, Millie swears they never did this in home school, either. So I thought of giving Floyd a lot more to do, too, since he seems to like being busy. I might put him on a much tighter schedule. Give him some goals and rewards. That would give him less time to think up new reasons to be mad at me."

"That sounds like a good plan. Have you tried talking to him about Hank?"

"*Tried* being the operative word. Yes. Twice. There won't be a third time. Learned my lesson. He was very grateful to us for letting Theo sleep upstairs, though, and that's helped a lot."

"Be careful with that."

"We are. Listen, I wanted to ask you about one more thing. I know it's a delicate subject but ignoring it isn't going to help. Lester said the plea bargain states that the boys have to go to you on April 1."

Daven braced himself. "I know, and I've been putting off mentioning it to you because I'd rather talk about it in person. Turns out that particular agreement was in writing after all. I saw it with my own eyes on Friday."

"Oh, shit. So we waited all that time for nothing. Doing nothing. I'm so sorry, Dav."

"Not your fault. Besides, neither of us knew Lester Boyd held the deeds, remember? I already asked Salome to override it, but the president said no. It's binding, Hank made sure of it. He couldn't have foreseen Floyd's objection to me. I'm appealing anyway, but it will fail and on April 1 they're mine for 19 years. I'm sorry, Rupe."

Rupert wasn't sure whether to be happy or sad about this news. "Okay, well...then we have about five months to change Floyd's mind about you."

"I'll be home Wednesday night, I think. On Saturday I'll tell him. No use keeping it from him and making him distrust me even more. That way he has those five months to come to terms with it."

"I think I should tell him."

"Why?"

"I just do. I'd rather him be mad at me about it than you."

"You have to live with him. Are you sure that's wise?"

"Trust me, Dav, please. I understand teenage boys about a million times better than you do at the moment. Let me tell him."

"When?"

"Now. He's out mowing the lawn. When he's done, I'll tell him we just got off the phone and that was the decision, and hope it instills a little trust that I'm keeping him updated every step of the way."

"Alright. If you're sure. Good luck."

Rupert didn't wait until Floyd was finished; instead he walked outside immediately after hanging up the phone and signaled him with a big wave to turn off the machine. Floyd set it to "quiet idle" instead, since it was a pain in the ass to restart, and waited for Rupert to reach him.

"Hey, Floyd. I just got off the phone with Daven. We need to talk. Or I need to tell you something, rather. You don't have to say anything if you don't want to. Will you come with me to the pool house, please?"

Floyd set the mower into an upright position and turned it completely off. "Funny how you act like I have a choice," he replied calmly, and started to walk towards the pool house.

Rupert froze in his tracks, his heart racing a little. Practically every encounter with one of the Bancroft sons was making a new grey hair sprout on his head, and it was wearing him out. They were so much like their father, although each in different ways.

"Floyd, come back here," he called in his normal tone.

Floyd stopped, a little confused, and walked back to Rupert with a quizzical expression.

"Let's try that again. Floyd, I have some news I'd like to tell you. Will you come to the pool house with me, please?"

Floyd said nothing, just stared at him blankly and crossed his arms.

"Okay," Rupert said after waiting a few long moments in vain. "You've been here ten days, and I've never ordered you to do anything once. I always ask. Always. Why are you suddenly treating me like some kind of evil dictator?"

"Because you keep framing your orders as a question in order to pretend I still have free will. But we both know I don't, so you acting like you're giving me a choice is just pissing me off."

Rupert swallowed hard. "I see. Thank you for being honest and giving us the chance to improve our communication. Go to the pool house, Floyd."

"Yes, sir."

"Thank you."

Floyd took the news completely stone-faced, which Rupert was actually thankful for since it was far better than almost any alternative.

"So...does this mean he can't free us?"

"I didn't say that. This is the contingency plan in case he can't. He's coming back to Los Angeles on Wednesday and will want to talk to you and Theo about the situation on Saturday."

"If he does free us, what then? We're still minors. Who will we live with? Will we have a choice?" Floyd's eyes were moist, and Rupert's eyes watered a little in response.

"Honestly, I haven't even thought about it. You'll have to ask Daven. One thing I do know is that my family is your family now, and if you have a choice, you can choose us."

"I don't want to choose! I just want my dad back."

That marked the immediate end of Rupert's fortitude; he started to cry silently and couldn't say anything more. Floyd watched him for a little while and felt his own heart seize up in response. Eventually he spoke up again.

"Sir...may I go now?"

Rupert wiped his eyes, taking a few moments to gather all his strength to get his shit back together before making a reply.

"In a minute. Floyd, you and I haven't talked about Daven at all. I promised I wouldn't make you talk to him, and I won't. But whatever I have to do to convince you he wasn't behind your dad's downfall, I will do it. I'll get the damned president on the phone if I have to. Just tell me what you need to help you get past this."

Floyd looked up, his eyes dry again. "I want to talk to Hailey Hendricks."

Rupert was startled into near speechlessness. "Hailey? Floyd, for god's sake. She's the one who caused this whole mess. No. Out of the question."

"You just said you'd do whatever I wanted. Do you have her number?"

"Yes, but....no, Floyd. Absolutely not. Don't ask me again. And while we're at it, I'm going to give you another order. Don't call me sir again. I'm Rupert. I'll tell Theo as well."

"Yes, sir. Rupert, I mean. I want to talk to Hailey. Right now."

"No. Go finish the mowing, and don't ask me again."

"No."

"No..?"

"I'm going to my room," Floyd declared firmly as he got up from the chaise lounge.

So much for that lack of defiance Rupe mentioned to Dav. He stood up now, too, and he was pissed. "Floyd, if you were one of my sons I'd already be getting the paddle out. Stop taking advantage of my promise not to, and do what I say. Outside. Now."

"Or else what?"

"That's not fair. You know I'm not going to do a damned thing, that's what. This situation is so fucked up, I'm the bad guy no matter what I do. Even when I'm trying to help you...it just...I can't understand." Rupert threw up his hands in surrender. "Do what you want, Floyd. But you're not talking to Hailey, ever, and that's final. It's for your own good."

Rupert left the pool house feeling like he was going to have a stroke from all the stress. He went to his master suite on the third floor and ran himself a painfully hot bath, hoping that Millie and the kids stayed out on their shopping trip for another hour or so.

When he heard them returning about 50 minutes later he pulled himself out of the bath - and out of his daydreams of being back in Maui with Dav and Hank - and hurried downstairs to see what help Chef needed with dinner, since he was certain Floyd wouldn't be showing up again.

He was surprised to find Floyd in the kitchen, quietly slicing potatoes and keeping a watchful eye on Theo's clumsy efforts to get all the right pots and pans heated up. Chef made his way over to Rupert.

"How are they doing, Chef?"

"Floyd might steal my job someday soon. Theo, not so much, since he doesn't try half as hard."

"That's alright, he's young. What are you guys making tonight?"

"Floyd asked to make beef wellington and cheddar potatoes au gratin. Is that okay?"

"Of course. You know that's my favorite meal. It was his idea?"

"Yes, he even had the nerve to insist on it." Chef chuckled a little. "Cheeky brat."

"Okay. That's good. Thanks."

Rupert went outside to put the mower away before the rain came. But it wasn't anywhere in sight, and all of the grass was cut.

He went into the garage instead, and sat down on a stool next to the mower and quietly "talked" to Hank about his boys. He might have cursed at him a little, too, for the hundredth time.

The days steadily improved as Rupert adjusted his style to try to keep Floyd happy. He gave the teenager a busier schedule, clear choices when he could, and clear orders when he couldn't. Even Theo was better and had started doing his chores without complaining. Most of the time, anyway.

That wasn't to say there weren't some tough issues to handle. Floyd had asked about Hailey twice more, and Rupert had calmly refused to discuss it. Each time, Floyd retreated into himself entirely, refusing to work until he snapped out of it many hours later. On one occasion, almost a full day. Rupert let him get away with it, much to Millie's dismay. She felt Floyd needed a firmer hand and that her husband was coddling the teenager, and she was right. But Rupert was tired of fighting with him.

He was also dreading the day that Daven would finally request to speak to the boys. He had been stuck in Philadelphia for another week, so there was no opportunity to try and get an in-person meeting together. Rupert knew he was dreading it more than anyone else; possibly including Floyd himself.

CHAPTER FOUR

One Sunday, between breakfast and lunch, the house phone rang and Floyd picked it up automatically as he was walking from the dining room into the kitchen.

"Aster residence.......hello?"

"Um. Hello Floyd, this is Daven. I need to speak to Rupert, but he's not answering his cell."

Floyd turned and eyed the cell phone that Rupert had uncharacteristically left lying out on the side table by the front door when he came home from church. It must be completely dead, Floyd figured.

"I'll go get him. Please hold."

"Thank-"

Floyd set the receiver down on the counter, then went to retrieve the cell phone so he could return it to Rupert for charging. He was surprised to see it wasn't dead, just on silent. He looked around furtively; no one was watching. So he slipped it into his pocket, then ran upstairs to find Rupert.

Floyd had sent Theody upstairs to play with the dogs, then locked himself in the basement bathroom, where he now sat on the closed toilet. His hand, which held Rupert's phone, was shaking violently. He had guessed the unlock code on the first try (the anniversary date, 12/31...so 1231). Now he just had to scroll through the contacts to find Hailey's number, and he hadn't yet found the courage to do it.

But when he finally did...there it was. Hailey Hendricks. Two phone numbers. Floyd called the first one; it was a disconnected line. He waited a minute to try the second one, feeling like he was going to vomit.

This one rang. And rang. And rang.

No answer after fifty rings.

Floyd scrolled back up and felt his heart stop again at the sight of Harmon's name. Without thinking, he hit "dial" and held his breath.

"Hello, Rupert. Thought we had an agreement not to call each other. Like, ever?"

Floyd felt like he'd been punched in the gut. He started to breathe fast. Too fast. Shit.

"Rupert?"

Floyd hung up and scrambled off the toilet. The phone lit up brightly, the screen showing "Incoming: Home." He quickly realized that Rupert was calling his own cell in an effort to find it within the house, and a few seconds after that call went to missed, the screen lit up again.

Incoming: Hailey Hendricks

In a panic Floyd hit the button to send the call to voicemail, cleared the call logs, and fled the bathroom to go back upstairs to replace the phone before Rupert could discover what was up.

Then the worst case scenario happened. Rupert was already in the living room, looking around in confusion, and he happened to turn just as Floyd came creeping through the door. Floyd froze as Rupert's eyes traveled down to his hand and widened in stunned comprehension.

"I'm sorry," Floyd said quickly, shakily, and he hurried over and handed him the phone. Unfortunately, Hailey Hendricks was calling back again.

"Interesting. Hailey is calling me. Did you talk to her?"

"N-no. I dialed her, b-but I chickened out."

"Wait for me in my office," Rupert ordered sharply, then he picked up the call. "Hello, Hailey. Yeah, sorry, butt dial."

"I'm sorry," Floyd mouthed before he turned away, petrified at Rupert's livid expression.

He slipped into Rupert's office, barely able to breathe. How stupid he had been! He couldn't believe himself. The man would have every right to say what he wanted now, or do what he wanted, and Floyd wouldn't even be mad. He deserved whatever was coming next, he knew without a doubt.

Rupert slipped into the office about fifteen seconds behind him, shutting the door quietly, but Floyd jumped at the clicking lock as if a gunshot had rang out.

"You called Harmon too, huh? Why?"

"I don't know. I chickened out with him also."

Rupert looked like he was going to slam the phone down on the table, but he collected himself just in time and laid it gently onto his big desk calendar.

"This is completely unacceptable, Floyd. It crosses a line I never thought you'd even consider, or be capable of."

"I know. I'm sorry."

"What do you think I should do about it?"

Rupert's face was like the worst thunderstorm imaginable, and Floyd shivered. He was suddenly ice cold.

"I think...I think you should..." He swallowed hard and composed himself, then felt his own anger building up quickly. "Whatever you do, it doesn't matter. I memorized Hailey's number, and I will call her when I have a chance, unless you chop off my hands and make it impossible. Then I'll just ask Theody to call her. Either way I'm getting an answer from her, whether you like it or not."

Rupert looked about to implode, but instead he took a few deep breaths and then sat down to think. Floyd watched him mull over the situation for a while, and was surprised when Rupert pulled his desk phone over to him, and calmly asked Floyd to sit down.

"Are you...are you calling her?"

"Yes. Afterwards, we'll discuss your punishment." Rupert punched the numbers quickly, and Hailey picked up on the first ring. Floyd's heart nearly stopped when he heard the voice. That same voice that had so confidently accused Daven of the ultimate treason.

"Is this a joke?" she responded without saying hello.

"No. This time, I really need to talk to you. I want you to tell me what proof you had in regards to your claim that Daven turned in Hank Bancroft. The story that you ran back on March...I guess around March 20."

"Oh, go fuck yourself. Lose my number, asshole."

She hung up, and Rupert raised an eyebrow at Floyd.

"That's Hailey for you. See why I didn't want you to call her?"

Floyd nodded. He was green. "Call her back. I'll talk to her directly."

"Are you sure?"

Floyd nodded again. Now he was white. "Do it. Please."

Rupert dialed back with a suppressed sigh.

"What the fuck, Aster? You suddenly got the hots for me, or what?"

Floyd swallowed hard and closed his eyes. "Ms. Hendricks? This is Floyd Bancroft."

There was silence, and it appeared Hailey had hung up. But then Floyd heard a car horn honking in the background, so he gathered his courage again.

"Ms. Hendricks, do you remember me from that day? When you gave me so much encouragement about my driving test?"

"Yeah. Yes, I do."

"Well, I never got to thank you. I passed it, you know, because you gave me the confidence to go through with it. So, thank you."

"Um. You're welcome? That's what you called me about?"

"No ma'am. I know you've heard the reports that I'm living with Rupert as his servant." Floyd's voice was hoarse. "I've been pissed off at Daven for months because I thought he turned my dad in. Because of your report, I mean. Now I'm being told he didn't, and it's making me a basket case. I just...I just want to know the truth. He used to be like a second father to me. I'm not mad at you or anything. Can you tell me if that report was true? Just a yes or no, and I'll never bother you again."

Silence. Rupert wiped his eyes with the back of his hand. Floyd had broken his heart so many times, it was a wonder it could still beat on its own.

"Ms. Hendricks?" Floyd said eventually. "You still there?"

"Yes. Didn't you get to read the FBI statement? Your dad allegedly turned himself in."

"I did read it." Floyd hated that his voice was shaking a little. "But I don't trust the FBI. And Daven didn't defend him at all. So I thought they were lying."

"Yeah, we all did, honey. We still do. Everyone who reported this story lost their journalism license, including me, because we were supposedly all wrong about Daven. There was no proof. But he did it, you just got to connect the dots and it all comes together clear as day. Rupert knows this already. Hell, everyone knows. You *should* be pissed at Daven. I would be if I were you."

Floyd looked at Rupert, stricken, then back at the phone. "Okay. I just wanted to hear it from you directly. You were so nice to me that day, and I guess I knew you wouldn't lie to me. Thank you for your time."

He reached over and hung up the phone, then sat back and glared at Rupert. "You should have let me call her way back when I first asked! Why didn't you?"

"Because she's a pathological liar, Floyd! The only honest thing I've ever heard her say in ten years was the part where she told you there was no proof that Daven turned Hank in."

"Yeah, I got that. I'm not a little kid, I know when someone's lying. You should have let me call her earlier. That was fucked up, man."

Rupert was confused now, and it took him a while to grasp what Floyd was saying.

"Wait, so...you *didn't* believe her just now?"

"No, of course not. For one thing, I started by asking her if she remembered encouraging me to take my driving test. She said yes, but that never happened. Jesus, how gullible do you think I am?"

"I never said you were gullible, Floyd. Mind your tone, please."

Floyd huffed. "*Everyone* lies to me. Everyone. The only person who has ever told me the truth all the time is my dad. I've become an expert bullshit detector in the past 8 months."

Rupert held his tongue with effort; he knew full well Hank had been dishonest with his sons on many occasions. Mostly to protect them, but also to prevent fights.

"I haven't lied to you, Floyd."

Floyd smiled without humor. "Yes, you have. You and Daven have known dad was dead for months. Know how I know? The night we arrived, your wife gave me her condolences, and said it had been a hard secret for you to hold in for so long. That you'd been working so hard to honor his legacy."

Oh, fuck....

"Floyd, I'm sorry," Rupert said quietly. "I can't defend that."

"No, you can't. And neither can Daven. So when you wonder why I have trust issues-"

"No, you're wrong about Dav," Rupert said quickly. "He never told you that. Lester and I did, without his knowledge. He nearly fired me over it, and he's still super pissed off at me. Ask him directly, he'll tell you the truth."

"Why did *you* lie, then?"

Rupert sighed, feeling completely foolish. "Ironically enough, it was to gain your trust."

"Nice job. Call Daven, please. I'll ask him. If he lies to me, I'm done with both of you forever."

Rupert held his breath as he dialed and hit the speakerphone function.

"Not a good time, Rupert," Daven answered tersely.

"Uh, make it a good time. I've got Floyd here with a question."

"How long have you known my dad was dead?" Floyd blurted impatiently.

They heard Daven excusing himself and a female voice answered; apparently he was in a meeting with Salome.

"Floyd?"

"Yes. Answer the question, please."

"I found out on...June 15."

"How long has Rupert known?"

There was a pause. "The same day. He was in Philadelphia with me when the FBI broke the news, and I told him when I got back to the hotel."

"And Lester? When did he find out?"

Now there was an even longer pause.

"Tell him, Dav," Rupert said quietly.

"Yes, trying to. I'm thinking. I honestly don't know if it was on April 1 or April 2. But one of those days. I'm sorry, Floyd. They shouldn't have lied to you. I don't support it, and I'm still really angry. It's one of the many things I wanted to tell you when we see each other again."

Then Floyd steeled himself and proposed the question Rupert was most afraid of, the one that could spin the poor kid into a nervous breakdown he might never recover from.

"Alright. So...I'm guessing he didn't die of a heart attack, either."

"Rupe, take Floyd over the house right now and give him Hank's death certificate. The real one, not the photocopy. The combination to his safe is 120949."

Rupert snatched up a pen. "Wait, say that again, sorry."

"120949."

"Okay, we'll head over. Any other questions, Floyd?"

"No. Wait, yes. Have you figured out if you can free us, yet?"

"Not yet. I'm in a meeting right now to discuss getting your dad's conviction overturned as a first step, but we haven't progressed very far. The fact that he pled guilty is causing huge issues that frankly, I'm not sure we will be able to overcome."

Floyd looked hopeful, regardless of that glumly doubtful answer. "Okay...well, good luck."

"Thanks, Floyd. I understand Rupert has told you the other news, about April 1."

"Yes."

"I know you're not happy about it, not that he even needed to tell me. I'm still trying to get that overturned as well so that you can stay with him. We'll talk soon."

"Okay. Thank you. Bye."

Floyd looked at Rupert as he hung up the phone, his expression stricken again. "I don't want to go to the house."

"You don't have to. I'll go get the thing and bring it back for you, okay?"

"No. I want to see it come out of the safe for myself."

Clearly Floyd's distrust of Rupert had grown exponentially in the past few minutes, not that he could blame him.

"Well, the safe is bolted into the wall. You either come with me, or I bring the papers to you, no other choice."

Floyd nodded. "Okay. Let's go."

Floyd completely fell apart as they pulled into the driveway, as Rupert feared he might. Toby, the current guard on duty, ran into the house and came out with Kleenex and a bottle of apple juice. Floyd went through an entire box of tissues and was just starting on a second one when the sky suddenly broke open and started drenching landscape. Rupert was glad for the roofed porte cochere that extended over the driveway and covered the car.

"Thanks, Toby. Help me get him inside."

"No, I'm fine," Floyd insisted as he sniffled. "Please, let's just get this over with. Hi, Toby. It's nice to see you again."

"You too, Floyd. Been a long time." Toby was red-eyed, too.

Floyd got out of the car and asked to open the safe himself. He didn't need to look at the paper as he punched in the number and swung the door wide open.

"I don't know where it is," he mumbled.

"I don't either."

Floyd pulled out a few large envelopes, reading the titles and then carefully setting them down on the desk as he reached in for more. He took out a powder blue one, about half the size of the others, and froze at what it said on the front.

"This is it," he said, sounding a little strangled. He didn't hesitate to break the seal and pull out the little certificate, but his hands were shaking. He scanned it for a while, then put it back in and replaced all the other envelopes on top of it and shut the door.

"I don't know how to lock this back up again."

"Want me to do it?"

"Yes, please."

Rupert went over and fussed with the door for a bit, not being familiar with the mechanism either. When he turned around, Floyd was gone, and Rupe found him standing in the middle of the living room.

"The house looks exactly the same," he said, sounding a little bewildered.

"Yes. Daven wanted to make sure you boys came home to how you left it. He didn't bring any of his own furniture or decor. Sold it all. Your rooms are as they were, too."

"It must be so weird for him to sleep in dad's bed."

"He doesn't. I doubt if he's been on the third floor even once since you left. He sleeps in the guest bedroom, or on the couch."

Floyd turned around to look at Rupert. "He sold everything else, though?"

"Yes. The other house, the boat, and the two SUVs. That's how he was able to afford freeing all of Hank's servants and paying the transfer fee for your deeds a couple weeks ago."

Floyd nodded again, clearly overcome but still managing to stay stoic, somehow.

"Did he sell Thunderbird?"

"No, he'd never do that. It's in the garage. Do you want to see it?"

"No. Let's go, please."

They drove back to the house in dead silence, but when they were parked, Floyd didn't move.

"What's on your mind?" Rupert asked.

"I was just thinking. I said earlier that everyone lies to me. That my dad was the only person who never lied to me."

"I'm so sorry, Floyd. I don't know how to make it up to you."

Floyd shrugged. "You can't. I was wrong, anyway. Dad did lie to us. He told us he was innocent. And he died in jail after admitting he was guilty. How long was his sentence? You never told me. Don't lie again, please."

"His record was sealed so we honestly don't know, Floyd," Rupert fudged. Better him than Daven, since he was already a lost cause in Floyd's eyes. "When they seal records like that, it's a life sentence 99% of the time. That's why Lester told you his passing was a mercy."

"The death certificate said heart attack, by the way. I'm sorry for not believing it."

"Don't ever apologize for any of this."

"Trust me, I won't. But I shouldn't have taken your phone. What's my punishment?"

"Nothing."

"Don't baby me. I fucked up, I can take it."

Rupert shook his head slightly. "I forgive you. Don't ever do it again, though. It would be nice if you stopped swearing so much, too."

"Okay." Floyd reached out for the door handle and started to tug it open, but stopped again.

"Rupert, don't take this the wrong way. You're my owner, so I have to treat you respectfully. But you should know that I really don't trust or respect you anymore. I don't want to be part of your family, and I actually want you to treat me like just a servant, as crazy as that sounds. So please leave me alone. If I need someone to talk to, I've got Theo."

Rupert felt his heart fall down to somewhere around his knees. "I hear you. It's not crazy, it's you setting your boundaries and I completely respect that. Let me be blunt for a moment, too: as long as you behave in a civil manner, we'll have no further problems. I can't, and won't, put up with all the attitude you've been giving me lately. I will start handing down discipline if necessary, because we can't continue like this. It's not healthy for you, and it's all been a terrible influence on your brother."

Floyd paused uncomfortably. "What kind of discipline?"

"I don't know," Rupert replied truthfully. "Let's not cross that bridge before we come to it. Even better, how about we avoid that bridge altogether?"

"Fine. Then I want to keep calling you sir. I'm not comfortable with anything else."
"If you insist."

"Thank you. One last thing. May I please stay in the car for a minute and borrow your cell phone?"

Rupert wanted so badly to ask who he was going to call. He feared the worst, naturally. Hailey. Or Harmon. Lester, maybe, although his number wasn't in the phone.

He didn't ask, however. He wanted to trust Floyd again, and had to start somewhere. Might as well be now. He took his phone from his back pocket and handed it over, then got out of the car.

"Rupert, *please*. I'm really busy. What now?"

"It's Floyd. I'm alone. Sorry to interrupt your meet-"

"Hang on."

"Okay."

Floyd's heart was pounding a little, and he almost hung up while waiting for Daven to come back on the line. It seemed to take forever and a day.

"Sorry, Floyd. Please continue."

"Um, hi. I just...you said you're trying to get the thing overturned. The April 1 thing, I mean."

"Yes, I made a little headway on it already. It's not as high of a priority as the other goal, to be honest, but it's far less complex. A matter of one simple legality to overturn, rather than a few dozen."

Floyd took a deep breath and smiled a little to himself. One thing he had forgotten that he really liked about Daven was that the man was incapable of being condescending and therefore treated everyone as intellectual equals, which always made Floyd feel a lot smarter and more worldly than he really was.

"Yeah, about that. I actually wanted to ask you to, um…to stop trying."

There was a puzzled pause on the other line. "You mean stop trying to overturn the April 1 decree?"

"Yeah. I meant that." Floyd suddenly felt ridiculously shy and awkward. "If it's okay with you, of course, and not too much trouble."

"If I remove it from the docket, I can't put it back again."

"That's fine."

Another pause, shorter this time. "Floyd, that means you and Theo will be transferred to my custody on April 1. I know you understand that, but please confirm this is really what you want before I proceed."

"Confirmed."

"Okay. Consider it done. Anything else?"

"No."

"Alright. One of us has to tell Rupert about this. I'll do it if you don't feel comfortable."

Floyd couldn't have been more grateful for that offer, and knew then he'd made the right decision. "Yeah, please tell him. He'll understand. When are you coming back to Los Angeles?"

"I wish I knew. It could be as early as Wednesday, but probably Friday. I'm afraid Shannon is going to forget who I am in the meantime."

"She won't. Starsky and Hutch didn't forget me and Theo and all, and that was like seven months."

Daven chuckled a little, which surprised Floyd slightly.

"That's good to hear. Alright, well, I'd better get back to it. Lots of ground to cover still, and it's getting late."

"Okay."

"Oh, and Floyd? I don't know what changed your mind, and won't ask. But I'm really happy that you did, all the same."

"Me, too. See you soon, Uncle Dav."

CHAPTER FIVE

Daven had never been more exhausted in his life as he climbed aboard his chartered jet for the flight back to Los Angeles. Three weeks of meetings in Philadelphia had steadily sapped every iota of energy he had left, which wasn't much to start with. Now he had a bad cold and a boat load of bad news to take home with him.

He felt guilty for not having kept in touch with Rupert at all, not even having called him for five days, but there wasn't much he could say about the FBI's stubborn and inexplicable reluctance to move on Yannick and Colbert. The only good news he really had was that he was merely fined for breaking the confidentiality agreement, and it was a fairly small amount considering the offense. There was no mention of any legal trouble, and he was stunned to find that he actually could get along with the president really well; he had shown himself to be a surprisingly forgiving man.

The caveat for this forgiveness, however, was that Daven was required to stay on as leader as the Seditionists for two more years in order to avoid destabilizing the nation's political world if the Urbanes went down. He'd accepted readily, pretending to care deeply about such stability. In reality, he just knew that if he left the party now - when he was *finally* being listened to by the president - his influence in Colbert's investigation would plummet to exactly zero.

Rupert would be thrilled, of course. That's exactly why Daven hadn't told him yet, because he didn't want to hear what great news it supposedly was. There were the boys to think about now; he was going to need to find ways to cut his workload dramatically in order to avoid following Hank's footsteps as an absent father.

No. *Owner*. Not father.

"Sir?"

Daven looked up from his seat, then dutifully buckled his seatbelt. "Sorry. I need a drink before we take off, please. Something strong."

"We have Jameson Irish Whiskey onboard, and Grey Goose."

Daven's brain jolted a little, the coincidence making the hair on his arms stand at attention. Both of those drinks had been Hank's adult beverages of choice on the rare occasions he indulged. *Overindulged* , rather - Hank never did anything halfway, and his resulting hangovers had been truly spectacular to witness.

"Actually, I'll just take some water. Sparkling if you have it."

Daven pulled out his phone as she walked away to call Rupert, but there was no answer. So he dialed Hank's cell phone, which had never been disconnected for some reason, just to listen to his voicemail message again. He wasn't sure why he did that every few days, and had been determined to stop, but he couldn't help himself.

"Dav. Wake up!" a deep voice urged.

"What?"

"We're crashing. Got your seatbelt on? We're going down."

"Hank?! What the hell? How...HOW are you here?"

Hank shrugged. "I don't know. But we're going to crash if you don't level out."

"Level out? What do you mean?" Daven asked coolly. "Wait. I'm dreaming, aren't I?"

"Yeah." Hank smiled. "You got me. I was just testing you. You believed we were crashing, didn't you? And you were actually glad. Relieved, even."

Daven gulped audibly. "So...we're not crashing?"

"Nope. Disappointed?"

"Yes. Wait, no...I don't know. That's strange, isn't it?"

"Hm. How about if I tell you we're not the only ones on this plane?"

He jerked a thumb behind him, and Daven turned around to see Floyd and Theo standing in the aisle, looking petrified.

"You go down, they go down, Dav," Hank said sternly. "You got to level out and get some altitude. Mountains ahead. Brace yourself."

Daven jerked upright with a gasp, suddenly fully awake, his neck aching from leaning up against the window for so long in the cold airplane cabin.

Rupert Aster was having a horrifically bad day at the office. Not only had the news of the boys being servants at his house gotten out - for which he wanted to blame Hailey even though there were dozens of other people who knew - but somehow word had leaked that Colbert was under investigation. Rupe had all but flipped his lid when he found out at breakfast, scaring the boys with his rare temper (all of them, including his own) and setting his poor wife on edge yet again. To make matters worse, Daven was completely unreachable due to his travels back home, and Salome was refusing to take his call.

In short, Rupe was ready to quit and go hide under a rock for the rest of his life. It certainly didn't help that it was Employee Appreciation Day at the office, which provided unnecessary distraction and sucked up all the time he could have been using to field dozens upon dozens of media inquiries.

And now, just as he was making headway on a media statement, his wife was calling to let him know that Floyd had disappeared. Rupert immediately raced home in a panic.

"Floyd, this is it. This is the last straw. I told you there was going to be discipline from now on, so here we are." Rupert's voice was at normal volume, but he was pissed and there was a significantly dangerous edge to it.

"I was only gone for like twenty minutes!" Floyd argued, not listening to a word.

"Forty-three minutes exactly. Where were you?"

"I went for a walk. The gardeners left the side gate open. Nobody saw me!"

"In the corner, Floyd. Forty-three minutes, same amount of time you were gone; or until you decide to tell me what the hell you were thinking. Your choice."

"Rupert-"

"Oh, *now* it's Rupert? Go. I'll be sitting right here, working on the project I had to abandon in order to race home to find you."

Floyd went. He only lasted four minutes before he turned around and quietly asked to speak.

"Yes, *please*," Rupert huffed. "Anything is better than the silent treatment you've been giving me all week."

Floyd didn't look straight at Rupert; just slightly off to the left. "I'm sixteen years old. Almost seventeen."

"Okay. You're upset at getting a little kid's punishment, I understand. Since you know you best, how do you suggest we handle this?"

Floyd swallowed down the lumps in his throat. "No, that's not...I wasn't trying to get out of it. I'm *sixteen*. I should be in high school right now, kissing girls and giving you headaches for reasons other than just going for a walk. Smoking marijuana, ditching class, whatever. I'm going crazy being locked up here. This is so fucked up!"

"I know, but-"

"You know what's even worse?" Floyd continued quietly, but his voice was now tinted heavily with anger and accusation.

"This law that put me and Theo here as your slaves? It's *your* fault for promoting it in the first place. And Daven's. So don't expect me to be grateful to either of you for anything. *Ever.*"

Rupert felt himself rapidly getting smaller as his indignation deflated, while also taking note of the fact that Floyd apparently didn't include his own dad in the reasons for his hostility. Rupe didn't really trust himself to reply for a few moments without his voice cracking, but Floyd was waiting expectantly, and this was the first time he'd been open about his feelings.

Say something, you idiot. And don't cry.

"You're not my slaves," he replied carefully. "And you *know* Daven is doing everything in his power to change the situation. You have every right in the world to be angry, but I'm begging you to be patient."

"He won't be able to do a damned thing."

"Not for lack of trying. I want to remind you, Floyd, like it or not, that despite my position you'll get arrested for being unaccompanied in public. That means transfer to state custody and manual labor. So you *will* stay on these grounds at all times, end of story. And I *will* reinforce that rule with whatever means necessary if you so much as set a toe outside the gates again without a pass. Is that understood?"

Rupert had harshly barked out this last part, and was satisfied to see Floyd react in an appropriately chastened fashion to the veiled threat. The teenager breathed deeply to himself as he crossed his arms, nodded, and stared at the floor silently.

"I'm sorry, Floyd. I hate yelling, and I really don't want to break the promise I made to you back at the school, but it was incredibly selfish to leave like that. Think of your brother. Do something stupid else stupid and you'll get separated, and I won't be able to do a damned thing about it. Is that what you want?"

"No," Floyd replied quickly, without hostility.

"Okay, then. Let's put this behind us and move on. Listen, Dav is flying home right now. If you'd like, I'll invite him over tomorrow and you two can go out to the pool house and talk. As long as you need. Would you like that? I assume you'd prefer that over going back to your own house."

Floyd nodded again, his heart warming by a few degrees at the pointed reference to *his* house.

"Okay. I'll arrange it with him. Look, no matter what you say, you're part of my family. I love you, and I want you to be safe and as comfortable as possible. The security at this house is for my protection, not your imprisonment, but if-"

"I'm not going anywhere as long as Theo is still here," Floyd interrupted hoarsely.

"Good to know."

"May I go back to the corner now?" Floyd was done talking; his fists balled back up and his expression hardened again. But it had been a good start, Rupert knew.

"Wait. I just realized the dogs haven't been out to play today at all. Are we just going to keep neglecting them like that on a beautiful afternoon like this?"

"Beautiful? It's been raining sideways."

"Eh, just a few sprinkles now."

Floyd glanced outside. "Yeah, but the sky is *black*."

"Light grey. Don't exaggerate."

Floyd gave in now, realizing what Rupert was up to. The barest hit of a smile played on his mouth. For a fraction of a second only, yes, but it was definitely there.

"Should I take the dogs out to play now, before the storm starts up again?"

"What an excellent idea, thank you. Yes. I'm going back to work. I think I'd like bacon cheeseburgers for dinner, can you arrange that with Chef?"

There was a tentative knock on the airplane's lavatory door, and then Martinez's muffled voice.

Daven gathered himself quickly and exited, his face still glistening because he had run out of paper towels to wipe the water away. "Yes. I'm fine."

"I'm sorry, sir, I didn't mean to intrude. I was concerned-"

"Where are we?"

"I guess over Palm Springs somewhere. We're starting the descent. That's why I came back to-"

"Yes, thank you."

"Alright." Martinez shifted on his feet and looked a little sideways at him. "If you're going to be okay, I'll go back up front."

Daven walked back into the main cabin and looked at the seat next to his. "Sit down, if you don't mind. Right here. Please."

Martinez sat, looking more concerned than even a few minutes ago, but he said nothing and relaxed a little into the softness of the swivel seat. It was the same chair that Starsky and/or Hutch had chewed up, but since repaired, the leather seat now a slightly different color than the back and arm rests.

Daven took another long drink of water. "Look, I, uh...we were in Philadelphia for a long time. I think I maybe said fifty words to you altogether."

"I think closer to a hundred would be a fair guess," Martinez responded lightly. In truth, it really was closer to fifty. Maybe forty, all of which were probably '*let's go*' at the end of each day.

"I'm sorry." He really meant it, too, which surprised both of them. "Listen, I've been meaning to tell you something for a while. But I wasn't allowed to. The FBI is making a statement tomorrow regarding the status of Hank Bancroft. I know you were friends, and that he was close to your dad."

"Yes." Martinez nodded sagely; in truth, the only reason he had stayed to protect Daven - a man he secretly disliked - was because he promised Hank he would. This chat was the longest they'd ever had in one sitting already, and nothing much had even been said yet.

Daven took a deep breath. "I'm afraid I have some very bad news to tell you, and there's no use trying to soften it. Hank passed away. It's being made public in the morning. I'm sorry to break it to you this way, but I didn't want to...are you okay?"

Martinez wiped his eyes with his sleeve. "Uh, yeah."

"I'm sorry."

"No, it's good. I knew, anyway. I'm good, really…it's kind of a relief to just hear you confirm it, one way or the other."

"You *knew*?"

"Not hard to figure out when you guys are always talking about him in past tense."

"Oh." Daven was embarrassed, but it passed quickly. "I'm truly sorry you and I started off on the wrong foot and still haven't quite learned to walk yet. I appreciate your efforts more than I could ever express. And I mean that literally; I'm really, *really* bad at telling people how I feel about them. Thank you for staying with me even though I've given you exactly zero reasons to do so. I'm not a nice person, unfortunately."

Martinez couldn't really argue with that, considering the offhanded and aloof way Daven had treated him for months, so he didn't.

"Alright, so…where do we go from here? I don't mean you and me, I mean just everything in general. The party, and the kids. What happens to them?"

"I've accepted formal leadership of the party. As for the rest of it, I can't tell you, and it won't be included in the FBI release. On an unrelated note, I'm going to ask Avery to come back and work for Rupert and help take care of the boys now that their introductory period is almost over and they can start going out in public again. I've been trying to set up a conversation with him for a couple weeks, but he never responds."

Martinez was still wiping his eyes, but he was totally composed otherwise. "He's on vacation, so don't take it personally. Went on some backpacking trip for like three weeks. He'll be back today, I think. Or tomorrow. He always asks about you, you know. Always tells me to say hello."

Daven nodded, feel greatly relieved but also confused. He thought Avery hated him for some unknown reason, especially because the man had bowed out of two lunches they'd arranged, with little explanation. Daven hadn't invited him again.

"Great. Thank you. I'll call him in a few days and set up a luncheon meeting at his favorite restaurant. I'd be very pleased if you would join us. At the table and in conversation, I mean."

Martinez blinked in surprise. "I...are you sure?"

"Yes. No obligation, of course. I wouldn't blame you for declining, considering...well, everything." Daven waved his hands around vaguely, then stared out the window, already lost in thought again. "No need to answer now," he added absently.

The guard wasn't sure what his answer would be, but his heart glowed a little at the invitation anyway. He kept silent and thought about Hank for a while, and once again mourned the loss of the man who had singlehandedly reunited the Martinez family by taking him in as a new guard without hesitation after their first meeting. It was so hard to understand why he was gone.

CHAPTER SIX

"Sorry I missed you earlier, Dav, what's up?"

With all the background music it sounded like Rupert was at a party, and Daven glanced at his watch. It was 3:30pm here in Los Angeles, on a Friday.

"I'm on my way home from the airport. What's all that noise?"

There was a slight pause. "Happy hour."

"Oh...okay."

"Been a bit of a week. You sound horrible. Are you sick?"

Daven grunted. "As a dog. I hate that saying, though. It makes no sense. I've never seen a dog with a bad cold."

"You know," Rupert said, ignoring the observation, "I've been waiting three freaking weeks for you to tell me what's going on. You've said nothing. Are you leaving us, or what? I don't even know if I can wait even one more minute until home you, get you...get home. I mean."

"Are you...are you *drunk?*"

"Had a few, yeah. It's been a bit of a week."

Daven sighed. "So I've heard. No, I'm not leaving the party. I was confirmed. There's literally nothing to tell you. The president can't make a fucking decision either way."

"Oh. Swearing. Yikes. Dav, um…"

"What?"

"The boys. I think we'll have to put Floyd in therapy again."

Daven nodded. "Sorry to hear. I'll pay for it, of course."

"You haven't asked about them lately. Like, at all. Not checked in once all week. Hank never asked about them either when he was away and that used to drive you crazy."

Pause. "He was their *father*. We'll talk when you're sober again. Who's with you?"

Rupert rattled off a list of about 19 people, and Daven closed his eyes in pain. All those colleagues, seeing Rupe drunk like that. It didn't bear thinking about.

"You should go home. It's not proper to…you know what, never mind."

"Mmmhmm. Hey, can you come over tomorrow and talk to Floyd."

"Actually, I was hoping I could come over now. Maybe since you're not home that might be an even better option."

"Yeah," Rupert said after thinking about it. "Call Millie and have her ask Floyd. I don't know if he's ready. He had a hell of a day."

"Oh. I'm afraid to ask."

"Probably best if you don't."

"Alright. Don't do anything tonight that's going to land you in the papers on Monday."

He hung up, then dialed Millie. Floyd wasn't ready, she confirmed after briefly consulting with the teenager. Maybe tomorrow.

So Daven went home and laid awake all night long.

Saturday Afternoon, 3pm

Daven said nothing much until he and Floyd were in the pool house with a couple of bottles of soda and a box of Kleenex. Theo had been happy to see him, of course, but despite his last heartwarming conversation with Floyd, it was abundantly clear that the teenager wasn't exactly thrilled with his return yet.

"It's good to see you again," Dav began as Floyd made himself comfortable on one of the big patio chairs that had been pulled inside the pool house for winter. "So sorry for being late. I've been on the phone with the FBI for hours today. I have a lot to tell you, but first things first. I haven't secured your freedom yet."

Floyd didn't seem surprised. "Okay."

"The good news on that front is that the answer wasn't no."

"I don't understand why you're even bothering. Dad was guilty, and this was our sentence. Why would they ever consider just suddenly letting us off the hook?"

Daven took a deep breath. Here goes. "I'm going to be honest with you Floyd. Now, and forever. The reasons behind that possibility are so unbelievable, that frankly, I can't even process it. If I can't, neither can you."

Floyd sat up a little, looking offended. "Oh."

"Secondly...Rupert knows you've been watching the news, but he doesn't say anything because he doesn't want to fight with you. I want you to stop. Promise me you will."

"Why?"

"Because a lot of stuff about your dad is going to get out soon, and most of it will be twisted into lies and be very disturbing to you. Rupert and I will keep you updated on the actual truth."

"I know about Colbert already. Saw it this morning."

"You know nothing about it from just that little blurb. Rupert told me about your call with Hailey."

Floyd flushed hotly, but said nothing.

"Things are about to get even crazier," Daven continued coolly, "and you only heard one piece of a moving machine of a thousand pieces we've been working on. Promise me you'll stop sneaking in to the TV room."

Floyd hesitated, then shook his head no.

Daven sighed, disappointed but not surprised. "Alright. Then let's move on. This next part is going to be very hard to hear, but I need you to be strong. If you're not ready, tell me."

Floyd glanced at the Kleenex box, then back to Daven. "Um. Will I ever be ready? Go ahead."

"Your dad didn't get a prison term. He was headed that direction, at least twenty years. Then something happened and he...he was sentenced to death."

"Okay. That makes sense," Floyd said calmly, his shaking voice betraying his placid expression and thudding heartbeat. "He said…"

Daven didn't prompt him, despite his immediate, keen interest in what Hank had said. Something changed the teenager's mind, though, and he waved his hand dismissively.

"I'm sorry, Uncle Dav. Go ahead."

Damn. "Alright, well, this is the worst part. I can't even fathom how I could possibly soften the news. Your dad, he really did have a heart attack. That was the legal cause of his death, and what they had to put on the certificate. But it was…it wasn't natural. It was artificially induced. By lethal injection."

"Uhhh." Floyd broke into a heavy sweat now, too, and his face was bright red.

"Do you understand what I'm saying?" Daven asked needlessly.

"Yeah. You know what, maybe I wasn't ready for this news after all."

"You're taking it very well, considering."

"Not really. Um…did you ever consider that maybe this was something you could have kept from me, that I would have actually been fine with *not knowing?*"

Daven shook his head. "No. I never considered that. No one on earth deserves the truth more than you. I will let you decide when we should tell Theo, if ever. Lester and Rupert know, but I basically told them I would kill them both if they didn't let me tell you myself. So don't blame them. If you're going to be mad at someone for that, it should be me."

"I'm not mad. But all that crap they said about him dying in his sleep, and no pain-"

"It was true. They fully sedated him first. He felt nothing, and I'm told he was in good spirits before that. Joking around, and not concerned about dying, at all. Which is, of course, so typically Hank."

It was, too. Floyd could picture the scene easily. He looked at his hands, then wiped his eyes with his sleeves again, but said nothing. Asked nothing.

Daven waited a while, then gently probed. "You mentioned a few moments ago that your dad said something to you. What was it, exactly? It might help me."

*

I chose this, Floyd. Don't blame anyone else. I'm content. Take care of your brother, and be really good for Dav. I love you. We'll be together again someday, and none of this will matter.

*

Floyd had thought he meant it literally - as in, *we'll be together again in maybe ten or twenty years and move to a cabin off the grid in Yosemite,* or similar. The idea that he meant another thing entirely - something otherworldly - had never occurred to the teenager. Not even *once*, until this very moment.

The words were meant for him alone, and no one else. Gently murmured into his ear within sight of the FBI, but not within hearing. Their lives had been so public, so exposed, so open for interpretation by strangers, that this parting reassurance was the only secret they had left to share between the two of them.

And it was going to stay that way.

"No," Floyd replied to Daven in a near-whisper, multiple streams of tears now trickling down his face. "It won't help you. But it helped me."

Daven handed Floyd the box of Kleenex. "I feel like I should leave you alone, even though I don't want to. Is that what you want?"

Floyd nodded and sniffled, then looked up at the sound of something suddenly raking against glass. He peered around Dav to the pool house door, where a familiar face was staring at him intently, paw pressed flat against the screen.

"Shannon's here!" he yelped, a little startled.

"Yes, I asked Rupert to go get her. Want me to let her in?"

"Of course!"

Daven squeezed him on the shoulder and got up to open the door. Shannon came bursting in, sliding a little on the tile, and nearly knocked Floyd to the ground in all her unabashedly canine exuberance.

Daven shut the door and went back in the house, where Rupert was waiting in the kitchen impatiently, and angrily, for any kind of news from his boss.

"I told him about the execution," Dav said flatly as he picked up an orange from the fruit basket and stopped at the island to peel it.

"Oh. Shit. You didn't tell me you were going to-"

"Well, I did. So that's over with. Don't mention it to him, obviously, best to leave it alone."

"You *think?*" Rupert was stunned. "Alright. Change of topic, then. Colbert was arrested last night."

"I know," Dav replied calmly. "We should go into your office."

"Of course you know," Rupert continued without a pause as walked them down the hall and opened the heavy door for them both. "And then Harmon sent out that incredible statement this morning. What in the holy hell went down in Philadelphia? You said yesterday afternoon nothing was moving along, next thing I know I'm waking up to a freakin' overnight political apocalypse. You've got one a hell of a poker face, Dav."

"Thank you, I think. But I wasn't lying. They were all at a stalemate when I left, so I'm just as surprised as everyone else. The president couldn't make a decision on anything, and I was about to stroke out from the stress, so I insisted they let me go home for a few days to catch up on work, since you've been the running the place by yourself. Thank you for that, by the way. But then..."

Daven told the story of everything that happened after that, all occurring within the past 18 hours. Rupert couldn't believe it, but then he could…and then he couldn't again. Turned out Harmon himself had finally lost his patience with the pace of the investigation, threw up two middle fingers to the president, and took matters into his own hands.

Even more noteworthy, he had done it *publicly*. He started with a damning press release and media statement at 4pm on Friday, shortly after which Colbert was taken into custody in front of his entire staff. Harmon, of course, was immediately relieved of his leadership position by the president himself for interfering in an official investigation, but he had planned for that.

So now Colbert was in jail, long before his time was due (or well after, depending on one's point of view), a fact which, on the surface, seemed destined to derail the investigation so thoroughly that all the evidence tracks carefully laid down would be completely obliterated, a smoking trail of wreckage left strewn along them. Harmon had planned for that too, of course. He had learned a lot from Hank without even meaning to.

"Witness tampering? Are you fucking kidding me?" Rupert exclaimed as he stormed around his home office in a fit of enraged disbelief. He was exhausted already, and it had only been about ten minutes since the conversation started. "That's all they can pin on him? After everything he did?"

Daven stood placidly by the credenza, carefully peeling a second orange. "Calm down. Al Capone went down on tax evasion charges when they couldn't nail him on anything else. I'll take what we can get."

"Jesus Christ. Colbert will *maybe* get a few years in jail. Which witness is claiming it?"

Daven smiled beatifically and popped a wedge of orange in his mouth. "That's the best part. Harmon is claiming Colbert tampered with *him* and induced him to file false charges."

"Jesus Christ," Rupert repeated, stunned. "How the hell are you so calm right now?"

Daven shrugged. "Because it gets even better. Turns out Harmon was in cahoots with Yannick the entire time I was in Philadelphia. Before that, actually. Ever since we met in Temecula when I confirmed he was our mole."

"Oh, wow. Wait....you did *what* in Temecula??"

"Never mind. Anyway, Harmon got a hold of him and tipped him off, without the FBI knowing. Told him Colbert had done him dirty, and apparently befriended him instead of threatening him. I'm not sure of the details on that yet. So Yannick agreed to reconnect with Colbert and start recording the conversations. When they had enough to go on, Harmon pulled the fire alarm. Now the FBI can't possibly stall or hide the investigation any longer."

"Shit. They must be pissed."

"Let's just say today's calls contained more obscenities than I've ever heard in my life, on all occasions combined. Even Hank would have blushed."

Rupert was speechless when Daven smiled again. *Smiled.* Genuinely. *Twice in one day.*

"Alright. So...what do we do now?" Rupe asked, shaking his head in amazement.

"Nothing. These oranges are amazing, by the way. Where'd you buy them?"

The weekend was a veritable bloodbath for the Urbanes. The Seditionists said nothing, responded to zero requests for statements, and Daven made the decision to close the office for the upcoming week. Then he actually shut off his phone and his computer, and stayed in bed with Shannon for two days straight. Thanks to all the Nyquil he needed to fight his cold, he slept fairly peacefully through the entire ordeal.

This was contrary to Rupert, of course, who monitored every word said or written about the affair and drank a entire six-pack of Red Bulls in 36 hours to keep him going.

Seven weeks after the fracas began, it was over as suddenly as it had begun. Yannick had somehow gained immunity for his testimony and would get off scot-free, a fact which pissed off Rupert, Daven, and Harmon to no end. But they all knew that the man simply wouldn't have cooperated with the FBI otherwise, and they'd be back at square one without him. So they each quietly resolved to find peace within themselves for the compromise. Some things you just couldn't fight.

Harmon received a two-year sentence in a minimum security facility for his part in the affair, which basically amounted to gross negligence and violation of public trust for being totally oblivious in regards to the actions of his right hand man. He would have received more if he'd been implicated in Janet's murder, but nobody was. There simply wasn't enough proof of anything, and Colbert had at least been smart enough to not be recorded talking about it. But the Urbanes Organization was found culpable anyway in a separate civil lawsuit Daven had quietly filed on the side, and eventually were ordered to pay multi-million dollar settlements to both Janet's family and the Bancroft sons' trust funds.

Colbert got 3 years in a nasty federal prison for witness tampering after the hung jury argued for three weeks over the other alleged crimes, the charges for which were eventually dismissed. They simply couldn't buy all of Yannick's claims after multiple witnesses had thrown reasonable doubt upon his integrity and motives. And they weren't wrong.

It didn't matter in the end, though. Colbert was brutally shanked in prison six days into his sentence by another inmate, and was left to die alone, gasping and panicking, his hands cupped full and overflowing with his own blood and vomit.

Harmon had planned for that, too.

EPILOGUE

March 2, 2019

Johansson House

"Floyd?" Daven poked patiently at the teenager in his bed for the third time, then shook him a little. Nothing. He waited a moment longer, and then pulled the covers off without mercy once he remembered Hank's stories of what it took to get the kid up.

"Mmmphhm," he mumbled as he turned around and cracked open one eye.

"Hi," Daven said gently. "Do you know what day it is?"

Floyd startled a little, then sat up quickly, rubbing his bleary eyes. "Yes. Sorry, I'm up."

"Can you be ready in fifteen minutes?"

"Yes, sir."

"Please don't call me sir anymore. We talked about this."

"I know, sorry. I'm up."

"Okay. See you in the garage in 16 minutes."

Daven smiled, then went downstairs to find Theo, who was putting the collars on the dogs and refilling their water bowls. He was ready to go, of course, so Dav turned and headed down the stairs and into Avery's office. He and Brittany were there, chatting happily and sharing cinnamon banana bread that Floyd had made the night before.

"Hey boss."

"Ready to go, Avery? Big day."

"Been ready for about a year. Let's do it."

The quartet gathered in the garage, where Floyd was trembling slightly from nerves. The 17-year old pulled his hoodie tighter around him, and wolfed down another bite of the bacon breakfast burrito Chef had made especially for him.

"You ready, Floyd?" Daven asked quietly. "Theo?"

They nodded, so Daven closed the door and locked it behind him using the new fingerprint panels he'd insisted be installed on every door to keep Hank's sons extra safe.

"Okay, Avery. Let's get this little parade started, then. Boys, into the car."

Avery grinned, then went out to meet up with Martinez to get the SUVs positioned in the driveway.

Daven put the key into the ignition, then turned and regarded his best friend's sons fondly. "Happy Freedom Day. Today is going to be a bit of a circus, I'm afraid. But you already know that."

Floyd smiled a little, his eyes slightly moist. "Yeah. I don't think I'm going to mind all the cameras for a change. Let them look!"

"Don't go and become a ham on me, now," Dav joked as he backed the car out and waited for his guards to position their SUVs in front and in back of them.

Twenty minutes later the little procession - at first surrounded by news vans from every TV station within 200 miles - pulled by itself into a parking lot which had been closed and cleared out for the morning just for them, even screened from view of the street with black netting similar to the kind used for film shoots. Daven pulled through into that private area, closest to the building, then he and Theo got out.

Floyd swallowed down the last of his burrito, slid over to get behind the wheel, and poked his head out the window.

"Okay, guys. Here I go. Wish me luck."

"You don't need luck. You've had enough practice. Just remember to take it easy with those brakes, you were still too hard on them yesterday. What did I tell you is most important to watch out for?"

Floyd sighed a little, but it was all in good humor. "Pedestrians and bicycles. I know. Got it."

"Good. Alright then."

Daven walked away to greet the DMV manager to chat with him for a moment and give him a check. Then the man got into the car with Floyd and buckled in. Daven, Theody and Martinez all stood back to wave him off and shout good luck, despite Daven's claim that he didn't need it, while Avery climbed back into the SUV.

Floyd grinned, then turned his attention into the car and keyed the ignition.

That rumble.

Oh my god. Dad...I wish you were here to see this.

He got sad for a moment until he remembered his dad *had* been here to see this. It had been one of the man's proudest moments. And now Floyd would have the memory of Daven here to see it, too.

In reality, Dav could have easily turned in the paperwork for Floyd's old license to be reinstated, which would have taken all of three minutes, but he'd insisted on a new test to make sure Floyd was ready. Again. But Floyd didn't mind; he was pretty sure Dav also just wanted to be here for this event and make a memory of his own, on this first day as a second father and freshly retired former leader of the Seditionists.

"Okay," the instructor began. "Take a right out of the parking lot, Floyd. We'll go about half a mile and turn left."

Floyd's heart glowed as he pressed the accelerator just the right amount in order to pull out of the parking lot without lurching, and drove carefully down Santa Monica Boulevard, tailed closely by Avery's huge black Escalade...which in turn was quickly followed by overly-eager news vans.

Floyd ignored them all and sucked in a surprised breath at the sight before him. The ocean seemed an impossible shade of blue today, and somehow stretching into the sky farther than the horizon should allow. The trees whizzed by three times greener and brighter than he remembered, the pedestrians all absurdly radiant in their colorful spring attire.

It was utterly dazzling.

"I'm going to pretend you didn't just roll through that stop sign," the instructor said quietly. "Turn left at the second light."

Floyd quickly wiped his eyes as he flipped on his turn signal, then hesitated.

"I'm sorry, sir," he said quietly. "For the stop sign, too, but...can we go straight for a little while longer?"

To the ocean, he meant. As far away as he could get right now from what lay behind him. The instructor smiled a little; Daven had quietly asked him to give Floyd some leeway from the normal test route, within reason of course.

"Sure. Just mind the signs and keep up with the traffic. Going a bit too slow at the moment."

Floyd smiled now too as the light turned green and he undid the turn signal and pressed the accelerator again; more firmly this time. *There. That's better.* The Thunderbird purred contentedly at the faster speed, and Floyd's eyes glistened again as he patted her gearshift lovingly. He changed lanes once, then again, then confidently ramped up to meet the speed limit.

"You seem a lot more comfortable already. That's good," the instructor declared happily. "I think you're going to be fine, Floyd. You've got this. Just pay attention, keep your eyes on the road."

Floyd was starting to grin broadly, and he nodded in response, but he didn't actually hear the man's words at all.

"Yeah, I've got you," he was gently murmuring into the steering wheel. "I've got you. We've got this. We're going to have so much fun. Just you wait..."